SNOW TOWARD EVENING

A Year in a River Valley

SNOW TOWARD EVENING

A Year in a River Valley / Nature Poems Selected by Josette Frank

Paintings by THOMAS LOCKER

A PUFFIN PIED PIPER

PUFFIN PIED PIPER BOOKS
Published by the Penguin Group
Penguin Books USA Inc., 375 Hudson Street, New York, New York, 10014, U.S.A.
Penguin Books Ltd, 27 Wrights Lane, London W8 5TZ, England
Penguin Books Australia Ltd, Ringwood, Victoria, Australia
Penguin Books Canada Ltd, 10 Alcorn Avenue, Toronto, Ontario, Canada M4V 3B2
Penguin Books (N.Z.) Ltd, 182–190 Wairau Road, Auckland 10, New Zealand
Penguin Books Ltd, Registered Offices: Harmondsworth, Middlesex, England

Originally published in hardcover by
Dial Books
A Division of Penguin Books USA Inc.

*The art for each picture consists of an oil painting, which is
color-separated and reproduced in full color.*

SNOW TOWARD EVENING is also available
in hardcover from Dial Books.

In this book thirteen poets and the landscape painter Thomas Locker combine to invite readers young and old to enjoy nature's splendor through the changing seasons.

I have selected a group of poems each reflecting the feeling of one month. From his studio in the Hudson River valley, Thomas Locker watched the seasons change and developed paintings that capture the spirit of the poems.

It is our hope that this book will heighten and deepen the reader's feeling of closeness to nature.

—*Josette Frank*

January

·January·

The days are short,
The sun a spark
Hung thin between
The dark and dark.

Fat snowy footsteps
Track the floor.
Milk bottles burst
Outside the door.

The river is
A frozen place
Held still beneath
The trees of lace.

The sky is low.
The wind is gray.
The radiator
Purrs all day.

—John Updike

When Skies Are Low and Days Are Dark

· *February* ·

When skies are low
and days are dark,
and frost bites
like a hungry shark,
when mufflers muffle
ears and nose,
and puffy sparrows
huddle close—
how nice to know
that February
is something purely
temporary.

—*N. M. Bodecker*

Mountain Brook

· *March* ·

Because of the steepness,
the streamlet runs white,
narrow and broken
as lightning by night.

Because of the rocks,
it leaps this way and that,
fresh as a flower,
quick as a cat.

—*Elizabeth Coatsworth*

In Time of Silver Rain

· *April* ·

In time of silver rain
the earth
puts forth new life again,
green grasses grow
and flowers lift their heads,
and over all the plain
the wonder spreads
of life, of life, of life!

—*Langston Hughes*

Daffodils

· *May* ·

I wandered lonely as a cloud
that floats on high o'er vales and hills,
when all at once I saw a crowd,
a host, of golden daffodils;
beside the lake, beneath the trees,
fluttering and dancing in the breeze.

—*William Wordsworth*

Afternoon on a Hill

·June·

I will be the gladdest thing
Under the sun!
I will touch a hundred flowers
and not pick one.

I will look at cliffs and clouds
with quiet eyes,
Watch the wind bow down the grass,
and the grass rise.

And when the lights begin to show
up from the town,
I will mark which must be mine,
and then start down!

—Edna St. Vincent Millay

The River

·*July*·

Quiver shiver,
golden river,
   how you hold the sun!

Shimmer glimmer,
little waves,
   showing day is done.

—Charlotte Zolotow

Something Told the Wild Geese

Something told the wild geese
It was time to go.
Though the fields lay golden
something whispered—"snow."
Leaves were green and stirring,
Berries, luster-glossed,
But beneath warm feathers
something cautioned—"frost."
All the sagging orchards
Steamed with amber spice,
But each wild beast stiffened
at remembered ice.
Something told the wild geese
It was time to fly—
Summer sun was on their wings,
Winter in their cry.

—*Rachel Field*

· *August* ·

Mountain Wind

Windrush down the timber chutes
between the mountain's knees—
a hiss of distant breathing,
a shouting in the trees,
a recklessness of branches,
a wilderness a–sway,
when suddenly
a silence
takes your breath away.

—*Barbara Kunz Loots*

· *September* ·

Wind Has Shaken Autumn Down

· *October* ·

Wind has shaken autumn down,
left it sprawling on the ground,
shawling all in gold below,
waiting for the hush of snow.

—*Tony Johnston*

Fly Away

Fly away, fly away over the sea,
Sun-loving swallow, for summer is done;
Come again, come again, come back to me,
Bringing the summer and bringing the sun.

—*Christina Rossetti*

Snow Toward Evening

· *December* ·

Suddenly the sky turned gray,
The day,
   Which had been bitter and chill,
   Grew intensely soft and still.
Quietly
   From some invisible blossoming tree
   Millions of petals, cool and white,
   Drifted and blew,
   Lifted and flew,
   Fell with the falling night.

     —*Melville Cane*

A New Year

Here's a clean year,
   A white year.
      Reach your hand and take it.

You are
   The builder,
      And no one else can make it.

See what it is
   That waits here,
      Whole and new;

It's not a year only,
   But a world
      For you!

—Mary Carolyn Davies

Acknowledgments

*Special thanks to Maria B. Salvadore,
Coordinator of Children's Services, District of Columbia Public Library,
for her invaluable assistance in researching children's poetry.*

The poem "January" is taken from *A Child's Calendar* by John Updike. Copyright © 1965 by John Updike and Nancy Burkert. Reprinted by permission of Alfred A. Knopf, Inc.

"When Skies Are Low and Days Are Dark" by N.M. Bodecker. Reprinted with permission of Margaret K. McElderry Books, an imprint of Macmillan Publishing Company, from *Snowman Sniffles and Other Verse* by N.M. Bodecker. Text: Copyright © 1983 by N.M. Bodecker.

"Mountain Brook" by Elizabeth Coatsworth. Reprinted with permission of Macmillan Publishing Company from *Summer Green* by Elizabeth Coatsworth. Copyright 1948 by Macmillan Publishing Company, renewed 1976 by Elizabeth Coatsworth Beston.

"In Time of Silver Rain," copyright 1938, renewed 1966 by Langston Hughes. Reprinted from *Selected Poems of Langston Hughes,* by permission of Alfred A. Knopf, Inc.

"Afternoon on a Hill" by Edna St. Vincent Millay. From *Collected Poems,* Harper & Row. Copyright 1917, 1945 by Edna St. Vincent Millay. Reprinted by permission.

"The River" from *Everything Glistens and Everything Sings,* copyright © 1987 by Charlotte Zolotow, reprinted by permission of Harcourt Brace Jovanovich, Inc.

"Something Told the Wild Geese" by Rachel Field. Reprinted with permission of Macmillan Publishing Company from *Branches Green* by Rachel Field. Copyright 1934 by Macmillan Publishing Company, renewed 1962 by Arthur S. Pederson.

"Mountain Wind," copyright © 1978 by Barbara Kunz Loots. Reprinted with permission of Barbara Kunz Loots.

"Wind Has Shaken Autumn Down," copyright © 1990 by Tony Johnston, reprinted by permission of the author.

"Snow Toward Evening" from *So That it Flower,* copyright 1926 by Harcourt Brace Jovanovich, Inc., and renewed 1954 by Melville Cane, reprinted by permission of the publisher.

"A New Year" by Mary Carolyn Davies.